Sienna's Secret

By Katrina Avant

This book is a work of fiction and does not depict
any person living or dead. The characters and events were
created from the imagination of the author.

SIENNA'S SECRET

Copyright © March 2013

Katrina Avant

Cover Design by LLPix.com

Chapter 1

Sienna Mendez paced around her spacious corporate office, lightly tapping a black onyx fountain pen trimmed in eighteen-carat gold against her cheek. She was trying to make some sense of her sudden legal issues. She thought losing her mother to a heart attack was stressful enough until she discovered Pilar Mendez had a secret—a multi-billion dollar secret.

#

It was the day after Pilar's funeral when she discovered her mother's secret holdings. Sienna was at her Pilar's lavish home, packing away her personal effects to be given to a local charity. She had just placed the last box near the front door when the doorbell chimed. She glanced at her slender platinum watch and noted that it was too early for the charity to pick up her mother's things. Moving towards the door, she casually checked her appearance in the mirror hanging in the foyer. Satisfied that she was presentable for visitors, Sienna opened the door to her mother's attorney, Anderson Stone.

"Anderson, please come in." Sienna moved aside, with a gesture for him to enter.

Anderson hugged her as he entered the spacious Spanish-styled home. "Sienna, I am so sorry for your loss," he told her, kissing her cheek. Anderson was Sienna's oldest and dearest friend from college. He had kept the wolves away, while she studied to earn her first degree.

"I saw you and Paige at the funeral. I'm sorry I was unable to speak with you before you left," she apologized with a slight smile. The church had been filled with her and Pilar's family and friends, making it virtually impossible for her to personally greet all who attended.

"Not a problem. I know you've had your hands full with Pilar's sudden death. How have you been?"

"Anderson, I am so overwhelmed right now. With Mama gone...Come, let's sit down." Sienna led him into the lavishly decorated sitting room. Pilar loved nice things and every item in the room displayed her exquisite taste; from the expensive one-of-a-kind Southwest rug that covered the copper-stained floor, to the hand-made imported furniture. After offering refreshments, which her guest declined, Sienna sat and waited expectantly for Anderson to reveal the purpose of his visit.

"Sienna, I hate to come at you with this so soon, but your mother left strict instructions to make her wishes known, upon her death," Anderson explained. "As you know, I was Pilar's attorney, so I'm here to execute her will."

Sienna sighed. Pilar was adamant about having her affairs in order, especially after her husband, Sienna's father, had died of cancer soon after she graduated from college. It was then Pilar recognized how quickly life could change and wanted to make sure her only child was well taken care of, as her husband had done for them both.

"I'm sure you know your father left you and your mother well provided for when he passed, but what you may not have known is that your mother had amassed a substantial amount of wealth on her own." Anderson had hoped Pilar would have shared this with her daughter before now. But like everyone else who knew her, she undoubtedly believed she had plenty of time to share the information.

"What do you mean?" Sienna was perplexed. Her father had left more than enough for her and her mother to live comfortably for the rest of their lives. She didn't understand why Anderson was inferring that there was more—much more.

"Sienna, your mother wanted to make a name for herself. After your father died, she realized she was only known as Ivan's wife and your mother. She wanted to be known for more than that. Don't get me wrong, she loved being your mother and your father's wife, but she wanted her own identity."

Sienna listened while Anderson spoke, wondering what her mother could possibly have done to claim a uniqueness that she felt Pilar always possessed.

As if reading her mind, Anderson continued with the answer. "Sienna, Pilar owned a cluster of high-end resorts in Negril and Montego Bay Jamaica, a total of five resorts to be exact. All five boast a five-star rating, mostly catering to some of the world's wealthiest clientele."

Sienna's jaw dropped at this disclosure. "Anderson, how is that possible? My mother rarely left the country and when she did travel, it was to Puerto Rico to visit relatives."

She was beyond shocked. Aside from her yearly shopping sprees and spa treatments, Pilar appeared to have never spent massive amounts of money, unless it was for a new car every few years or some extravagant gift for her daughter. Sienna couldn't imagine her mother purchasing a chain of resorts. With Anderson's eye-opening news, she was beginning to believe those supposed trips to Puerto Rico were actually trips to Jamaica.

"But why didn't she tell me?" she asked.

Anderson shrugged. "Why she kept this side of herself a secret, she never explained. I asked her many times if she should share her property ownership with you, but she always expressed that you would know in due time. I never thought she meant at her death," Anderson told her. He understood Sienna's shock, but the biggest surprise was yet to come—the value of the properties.

#

Learning that her mother owned and headed a multi-billion dollar corporation had been more than a surprise to Sienna. And now to realize that she was the sole heir to that corporation was heart-pounding, to say the least. Her sudden wealth was out of her range of expertise.

Sienna's PhD in chemical engineering hadn't prepared her for corporations and property ownership. Not to mention, she would have to fly down to Jamaica to claim her inheritance. Although Anderson was her mother's attorney, he was unable to handle the particulars of her situation. He had more cases than he could handle at the moment but recommended one of the top international attorneys to handle her affairs. Sienna was to meet with this new attorney, at the flagship resort of her newly acquired properties in a couple of days.

Anticipating a lengthy stay in Jamaica, she had placed her request for a leave of absence from her position with one of the top petroleum companies in the country. She was to leave the next morning, heading to *Sienna's Secret*; the name Pilar had given to her most prized resort. Sienna wanted to get acquainted with the place before she was joined by Anderson's colleague, so she planned to arrive a day early. She wanted to take her time to acclimate herself to her mother's success.

Drawing a deep breath, she tossed the expensive pen—a gift from Pilar—onto her file-cluttered desk. Picking up her phone, she dialed her travel agent.

"Emma? It's Sienna. Change of plans…I would like to leave this afternoon." Nodding, as if the woman could see her, Sienna listened as Emma spoke into the phone. Satisfied with the change in arrangements, she hung up.

Sienna placed her briefcase on her desk, stuffing it with files she wanted to look over while she was gone. After tidying up her space, and locking away confidential documents, she took a long look around the room. Although she knew she would be returning at some point, she had the oddest feeling that this was her last time inside the space that had been her work home since graduating from college. Dismissing the sensation, Sienna shrugged before turning out the light and closing the door.

Chapter 2

Matthias Bennett sat in the lobby of *Sienna's Secret,* people-watching. When he wasn't in court or mapping out legal plans for his clients, he often took his lunch and sat outside to observe the throng who traveled to and fro around him. Tonight he had the luxury of sitting in the lobby of one of the tropics most prized hotels.

He had arrived a few days early to get a feel of the place and to observe the major players unnoticed. None of the hotel staff knew why he was there. As far as they were concerned, he was just another tourist. Matthias had covered his tracks well, so no one would suspect who he was or why he was there until he had the opportunity to fully assess any problems that had the potential to delay his new client's transition of ownership. He didn't want to tip his hand to those who may be involved in any unscrupulous activity just in case he needed to correct them in the future.

In his years of practicing corporate law, there was never a time when he didn't encounter employees who had their hand in the cookie jar so to speak. And he didn't expect the Mendez Corporation to be any different. He just hoped, aside from the norm, any additional problems would only require simple solutions allowing him and his client to conclude their business in a timely matter.

In his effort to make that happen, Matthias had done his preliminary work before leaving the States. From his cursory observation, there were some slight discrepancies in a couple of the resort's ledgers, not to mention a hint of some other dubious activities. Even so, he predicted the issues could be resolved quickly in keeping on schedule for a smooth transfer to the deceased owner's daughter.

As he pretended to read an activity brochure, he watched as the hotel's lead man, Romaro Grey flirted with one of the hotel's staff members. According to his investigator's report, Romaro was definitely one who needed watching— and closely. Matthias could guess, if anything was amiss, this man had his hand in it up to his elbow.

Matthias studied the wiry man. He was of average height, thin, spindly even. His smooth dark skin seemed to glisten with what appeared to be some sort of oil. He noticed even though the woman he flirted with smiled, that smile didn't quite reach her eyes. In actuality, she appeared repulsed. She did everything in her power to keep a comfortable distance from him and in Matthias' opinion with good reason. The man's lecherous grin and busy hands all but said he was an ass. Although the man was very careful where he touched the young woman, Matthias still labeled him a creep.

Shifting his gaze from Romaro to a pair of long, shapely legs that had strolled into his line of vision, Matthias let his eyes travel slowly up to the woman's face; a face he recognized from the photo Anderson had sent him. So, this is Sienna Mendez, he thought. He watched her as she made her way to the front desk, closely followed by a grinning bellman, whose eyes were firmly fixated on Sienna's skirt-swaying hips.

Sienna Mendez was at least five foot seven without the four-inch sea foam green heels she wore. She was dressed in a tank top of the same green color, which accentuated her sun-browned skin and generous breasts, coupled with a cream-colored ruffle-tailed, hip-hugging skirt. Her dark auburn hair was thick and wavy, just grazing the tops of her shoulders.

Recognizing Sienna instantly, Romaro quickly scrambled around the desk to personally greet her. Matthias watched the lustful little man's eyes crawl over Sienna's body, with them settling longingly on her silk-covered breasts. This move didn't sit well with Matthias. He instantly disliked the man more than he had before Sienna's arrival. He was about to break his resolve of anonymity and teach the wretched man some manners when Sienna spoke up.

"Please tell me that you don't greet the guests the way you just greeted me," she angrily scolded Romaro through clenched teeth.

"I don't know what you—" Romaro started, only to be cut off by Sienna.

"And don't further insult me by pretending not to understand my meaning," she reprimanded.

"Forgive me, Ms. Mendez, I didn't mean to insult you," Romaro apologized with a frown of disapproval at being called out on his unprofessionalism.

Matthias recognized the disdain that appeared in the man's eyes. Instead of accepting the reprimand in humility, the arrogant little bastard decided to take the low road. Yes, he was for sure the one to keep an eye on, and Matthias was just the man to make sure Romaro stayed in his place.

After apologizing again to his new boss, Romaro excused himself and retreated to his office. Matthias watched, while the embarrassed desk clerk apologized profusely for her boss's behavior, as she handed Sienna her keycards and resort packet. Sienna smiled at the young woman, assuring her that her apology was unnecessary. After accepting her items, Sienna gave the woman another smile before heading to the bank of elevators with the bellman close on her heels. After witnessing everything he needed to see, Matthias rose to head to his suite. Instead of asking the bellman to hold the elevator took the next one.

#

As she and the bellman exited the elevator, Sienna shook her head. She couldn't believe the awful way the director had treated her. She would certainly make it a point to speak to her attorney about him. If it was her choice, he would at the very least be demoted if not fired from his position. She didn't need any employee who behaved the way he had greeting customers.

Sienna swept into her suite, while the bellman placed her bags in their designated spot. Her suite covered half of the hotel's top floor in the main tower. The other half was her mother's private domain, which Sienna learned Pilar used whenever she visited. Sienna hadn't the heart to take Pilar's living quarters. She knew there would be too much of her mother there. She wasn't ready to confront her grief.

After the bellman left, Sienna walked over to the wall of windows and stared out into the lighted view of the hotel grounds framed by the calming ocean. The view was breathtaking. She hadn't known what to expect, as her private car brought her to *Sienna's Secret*. When she stepped into the lobby of the hotel, she was in awe of the décor, the architecture—the whole beautiful package. As she looked out into the night, her eyes misted at the thought of her mother and the small empire she had built. Her mother was an amazing woman, more amazing than she ever knew.

When Sienna learned of Pilar's business, she had studied the various details of each resort, but nothing could have prepared her for what she saw. *Sienna's Secret* was astonishing. While perusing information on the other resorts, she learned that each had its own theme which catered to a different clientele.

Sienna's Secret was the crown jewel. The resort was all-inclusive as well as the others, but was strictly an adult's playground with lovers in mind. It boasted elegant private bungalows, private cruises for secret rendezvous, honeymoons, and anniversaries, along with designated private beach areas for nude sunbathing or intimate picnics. At *Sienna's Secret,* couples could play and enjoy as they liked without being disturbed.

Then there was *Pilar's Playground* which was planned and built with families with children in mind. This resort hosted water parks, and cartoon-themed attractions, among many other events that would appeal to any child or those who were children at heart.

Sangria Beach catered to those who wanted the look and feel of everything Spanish, from the music to the food to the Spanish-styled architecture. The hotel gave one the feeling of being in old Spain with a Mediterranean flair.

Crystal Sun Beach, located in Negril, was the resort frequented by the young adult crowd and was usually a big hit during spring break. There were daily beach parties, horseback tours, sunbathing and nude bathing in secluded areas, and themed night parties that ended when the sun came up.

Pilar had thought of everything, Sienna noted. She had even built a resort that catered to seniors. The *Daybreak Beach Resort* was a retiree's dream; with casinos, shuffleboard, night cruises, and 50s, 60s, and 70s dance parties after dark. There were day trips that took them all over the island to indulge in any activity that appealed to them.

There were many types and styles of cuisine and restaurants, from elegant dining to poolside open grills, along with island tours and excursions to fit just about every need at every resort. Sienna was in awe of what her mother had accomplished.

#

Matthias let himself into his suite. Tossing the keycard onto a nearby table, he made his way to the refreshment cooler for a bottle of water. Taking a long drink, he picked up the information packet he had on Sienna Mendez; flipping through it until he came to her photo. He took another swallow while he studied her face.

"Humph, this photo doesn't do the lady justice," he said to the room. He thought about those legs as well as the rest of her. Although he would never be as crude as Romaro Grey, he did appreciate the lady's good looks.

Sienna Mendez possessed a generous curvy figure. Her full breasts sat high, commanding attention from any red-blooded male who was still breathing. Her olive complexion added to her exotic features, boasting of her Hispanic heritage. Matthias thought of her full mass of wavy hair that begged to be touched, not to mention her full mouth that begged to be kissed.

Matthias swiped a hand over his face at this last thought. He was there to help the lady settle her affairs, not to fantasize about her in his arms, kissing her senseless. Still, he was curious about her. Nowhere in her profile was information about her relationship status. He knew she wasn't married, but beyond that, he had no clue. Matthias drew his hand down his face again, with the remembrance of why he was there and the fact that he didn't get involved with clients as a rule. Setting his mind back on track he prepared for bed.

Chapter 3

"Do you mind if I join you?" Matthias asked of Sienna.

Looking up at the stranger through her Dolce and Gabbana sunglasses, Sienna raised an inquisitive eyebrow at his forwardness. "And why would I want you to join me?" She asked in return. While Sienna waited for his answer, she gave him a close but discreet inspection.

"Maybe I should introduce myself and let you decide," he said. "I'm Matthias Bennett, your attorney Ms. Mendez," Matthias informed her with a slight smile, pleased that she found interest in him with her prudent assessment.

Finally smiling, Sienna removed her sunglasses. "Of course Mr. Bennett, you may join me."

Sienna took another sweep of the man, as he pulled out a chair to join her. Matthias was not at all what she expected. When Anderson said a well-versed and well-traveled attorney would be handling her case, she automatically assumed a much older and settled gentleman; not the young vibrant one sitting before her. She accessed his age to be mid to late thirties, far from the age she expected. Matthias was tall and very handsome, with a complexion of smooth cocoa. Donning sandals, colorful island shorts, and a pale gray tank top, she noticed his body was sculpted to perfection. No, he was certainly not what she expected at all.

"I see we had the same idea," Matthias spoke up, breaking into her thoughts, as he settled into his chair. "I'm glad I decided to arrive early as well," he continued while watching her study him.

He had decided not to wait until their scheduled meeting to introduce himself, especially after last night's encounter with Grey. He had searched several of the resort's restaurants that morning, in hopes of finding her having breakfast. He found her on the patio of the least crowded one, enjoying the tropical sunshine.

Sienna smiled. "I guess we did. I arrived late last night. I must say I was a little anxious to see what my mother had built," she told him while glancing around the beautifully decorated restaurant.

Bringing her gaze back to Matthias, she addressed him. "So Mr. Bennett, tell me, how do you know Anderson?"

Before he could answer, one of the servers came to take their breakfast orders. After the server left, he answered her.

"First off, please call me Matthias or Matt if you like, Ms.—"

Sienna shook her head. "Sienna, please," she corrected. She knew she would choose to call him Matt instead of Matthias. Matt was more casual and she wanted to be casual with this handsome man.

"Well Sienna, Anderson is married to my sister, Paige," he answered. "Even though we crossed paths several times due to our profession, it was Paige who managed to meet him formally after she was commissioned to decorate his business offices. So naturally, he and I became better acquainted after they married. Anderson is a good guy and a hell of an attorney," Matthias complimented his brother-in-law and he meant it. For him, his sister couldn't have chosen a better partner if she tried.

Sienna smiled. "He speaks very highly of you also," she informed him. "After he couldn't handle my affairs himself, he assured me there wasn't a better man to do the job than yourself. So, I am more than comfortable with you handling this for me. Anderson's opinions mean a great deal to me."

"If I may ask, did you know Anderson before he became your mother's attorney?" Matthias was curious to know if she and Anderson ever dated.

Sienna's smile widened at this. "Yes. You can say that Anderson was a lifesaver during my college years. I met him a few weeks after arriving on campus. One night I was studying in the library when a group of frat guys spotted me sitting alone and decided to target me for whatever reason. One of them decided to approach me and asked if he could join me. When I said no, he became aggressive and refused to take my no for an answer. Anderson happened to be watching the exchange from across the room and intervened. He made the guy back off. After that night, he became my self-appointed big brother."

"Yeah, that sounds like Anderson," Matthias admitted.

"We kept in touch over the years, and after he moved to Metro City and opened his practice, I jumped on the chance to recommend him to my mother to handle all of her legal affairs."

Matthias didn't know why, but he felt relieved at this disclosure. "So I take it you've met my sister?" He asked, just as the server brought their drinks.

"Yes. Anderson introduced us before they were married. I must say, your sister is a lovely woman. She is such a perfect match for him. And their beautiful son, oh he's adorable."

Matthias smiled, thinking of his only nephew.

"I'm sorry to hear about your mother," he told her, bringing the conversation back to why they were on the island. "Although, I never met her personally, her business acumen is well known to me. I assisted Anderson in setting up your mother's company, so I am aware of what's involved. Even though I don't foresee any major issues, I would like to hold off on the transition, until I have my team take a thorough look at the corporation's holdings—that's if you don't object," he added.

"I consider you the expert Matt, so whatever you think is best I will follow your lead. I must also inform you that I knew nothing at all about my mother's corporation before she died. And I know even less about how to proceed, so I am at your mercy."

"I promise I won't let you down," Matthias assured her before lifting his glass of juice for a sip. He noticed that she preferred Matt. He approved of her choice.

#

Romaro Grey stood across the patio and watched Sienna smile at the man who shared her table. He wondered who he was and what he said that made her smile so brightly. She only had a frown for him last night.

He thought the new boss would be a push-over compared to Pilar, who ruled with an iron fist, even from her home in the States. After his research found that Sienna knew nothing about the hotel business, he was certain she would be easily manipulated. Especially, after learning that Stone, the corporation's attorney, wouldn't be joining her on her visit.

But that was before he met the woman and before she had eyed him with contempt. It was then Romaro realized she would not be easily handled. Still, he hoped to quickly appease her and send her back to the States, leaving him in full control of the resorts—and his personal interests. But, he mused, if she decided to stay awhile, maybe he could satisfy her in other ways as well. His mind ran rampant with his unrealistic possibilities.

Chapter 4

After breakfast, Sienna returned to her suite to dress for the activities that she and Matt had planned for the day. They had agreed she would tour all the properties with him after explaining he preferred the staff not to know who he was until it was necessary. He wanted to conduct his inspections of the properties and books without hindrance from any of the employees. The less they knew the quicker he could get things done.

With her by his side, he would be able to gain access to the necessary paperwork without suspicion. The staff, especially Romaro Grey, expected her to examine the resorts' contracts and daily operations, but not her guest. They had decided the best way to continue with his anonymity would be to pretend to be a couple to deter any questions concerning his presence.

Sienna considered Matt's charade. She had never pretended to be involved with someone, so this would be interesting, to say the least. She did find him attractive, so it shouldn't be a stretch to get others to believe that they were a couple. The more she thought about the ruse the more she believed it could be fun to have an imaginary relationship with the handsome man.

Stepping into the huge closet, she chose a beautiful floral print sundress, with a pale yellow background that complimented her complexion. Donning the dress, she slipped on a pair of melon-colored leather sandals, which matched perfectly with her chosen attire. After sliding on a lightly tinted lip gloss, Sienna pulled her hair into a loose ponytail. Grabbing a small purse and sunglasses, she headed for the door. She would meet Matthias in the lobby.

Matthias checked his watch while he waited for Sienna. He had run up to his room to change into chinos and a short-sleeved, cotton button-down shirt. On his feet, he chose a pair of comfortable Robert Graham sneakers. Armed with his mobile phone and wallet, he had taken the elevation down to the lobby to wait.

Feeling eyes on him, Matthias glanced up from his watch to catch Romaro staring at him. He viewed Matthias with as much disdain, as he had Sienna the previous night. Romaro gave him one last glare before he turned his attention elsewhere. Matthias wondered what the man was thinking. He hoped his cover wasn't blown.

Thinking quickly, he had an idea when he spotted Sienna exiting the elevator. After she reached him, without warning, he pulled her into his arms and kissed her—passionately. Feeling a slight resistance, he deepened the kiss, hoping she would follow his lead and not give him away. After feeling her relax, he prolonged the kiss a few seconds more before releasing her.

"Ready to begin our day, sweetheart?" He asked her, just loud enough for Romaro to hear. Sienna plastered on a smile and nodded. Clasping hands with her, he led her outside to their waiting car.

"Thank you for playing along with me," he whispered. "Grey was eying me just before you arrived. I don't know if he's suspicious or not, but I didn't want to take that chance," he explained before they reached their car. Sienna could only nod as they climbed inside. She was still reeling from his incredible kiss.

"Where to?" The driver asked in his native accent. Sienna found her voice to give the driver their first destination.

Deciding to continue the charade, Matthias placed his arm around her, drawing her closer to him as he nuzzled her neck. Not wanting to seem resistant, after catching the driver spying on them in the rearview mirror, Sienna closed her eyes and leaned into him, raising her chin to give him better access to her throat. Grinning widely at the amorous couple, the driver turned his attention back to the road.

Chapter 5

"I hope I didn't offend you in any way." Matthias was beginning to feel guilty in his efforts to curb any suspicions. Sienna had been quiet since their ordeal had begun. After they spent the entire day touring the other resorts, with Sienna making her formal introductions to the staff, they decided to have dinner at Pier One on the Waterfront, one of Jamaica's popular restaurants.

Sienna lifted her eyes from her menu. "No Matt, you didn't offend me. But I must say you caught me off guard with that kiss in the hotel lobby," she told him, after placing her menu aside.

Matthias smiled. "I'm just glad you caught on. I'm sure we made a believable couple, don't you think?" he asked her with a wink. Not expecting an answer he pressed on. "I thought it was best to continue once we got into the car. This is a small island. It would have gotten around if we only appeared to be lovers at the hotel."

"I completely understand. It's not a problem." Although she seemed perfectly calm on the outside, Sienna's body was pulsating. Every nerve ending was aware of how virile this man was. When he was all over her in the car, she thought she would pass out from his touch. Her panties were still damp from his lips on her throat.

Matt was unlike any attorney she had ever met. Unlike his brother-in-law's mostly business demeanor, Matt was laid back, unhurried, and playful even. If she hadn't known who he was, she would never have guessed his profession. She decided she liked him and began to relax and enjoy his company.

"Well…in that case, I have a proposal," Matthias was saying, bringing her out of her assessment.

"A proposal?" she asked, with a rise of a perfectly arched brow. Maybe she spoke too quickly on the relaxing part.

"Yes. Since we've started this pretense, I think we should keep it up until the final papers are signed." Matthias paused before delivering the next detail of his proposal.

"Also, I think it would be a good idea if we moved in together…share a suite, while we're here," he proposed.

Matthias waited for her reaction. He knew it was risky for him to suggest they move in together. She didn't know him and he would completely understand her rejection of the unexpected idea. But he wanted their relationship to appear authentic to any inquisitive eyes, at least that was what he had convinced himself. After inhaling her scent and tasting her skin during their car ride, his mind had become muddled.

Sienna could only blink at this added suggestion. She was all for play-acting, but to share a suite with this man? She didn't think that was a good idea at all. He already had her body's attention from just the brief contact they'd already had that day. How would she be able to handle him living with her? It was one thing to be attracted to the man and to fantasize, but to be under the same roof together was quite another. She was just about to voice her objection when Romaro Grey appeared at their table.

"Excuse me, Ms. Mendez, I wanted to apologize to you once more for my deplorable behavior last evening. I assure you that it won't happen again with you or any other guest. I hope that you will accept my sincerest apology." Although Romaro spoke to Sienna, his gaze strayed to Matthias who was staring at him intently.

Sensing that Grey needed more convincing, Matthias grasped Sienna's hand possessively, casually caressing it while staring back at Romaro. His smirk let the man know that he was with Sienna in every way.

"I accept your apology, Mr. Grey," Sienna told him as she watched the visual dual between the two men.

Bringing his eyes back to an inquisitive Sienna, he responded, "Thank you, Miss. I promise to make your stay here enjoyable." Nodding at both of them, Romaro left them to their meal.

"I swear that man is everywhere. I wonder if he's following us," Matthias said this more to himself than to Sienna. He made a mental note to mention his suspicions to his investigator. If the man was skulking around, he felt more than ever that Sienna needed his protection. He did not trust Romaro Grey.

#

Sienna hugged herself as she looked out at the ocean from her private balcony. She couldn't believe she was sharing a suite with Matt Bennett. After Romaro Grey left their table, she felt as if she had no other choice. The man was watching them like a proverbial hawk.

After Romaro left, she knew it was inevitable that they would share her living space, but she had spoken her concerns anyway. Didn't he already have a suite in the hotel and what was he going to do about said suite without arousing the Director's suspicion?

To her surprise, Matthias had that all covered. Because he was there anonymously, he had his investigator checked in at *Sienna's Secret* under his name—Kobe West. Matthias was registered at one of the island's other hotels where Kobe was staying, leaving him free to roam *Sienna's Secret* without suspicion. All he had to do was move his things into her suite, which he had done two hours ago. Sienna was thankful she had taken management's suggestion to occupy one of the two huge suites on the hotel's private floor. At least they wouldn't be in close quarters.

Returning to her room, she heard Matthias speaking to someone on the phone, concerning some of the files they had gathered that day. From his tone of voice, he didn't seem pleased.

Immediately after placing his things in the other bedroom, Matthias had spread files out onto the dining table, while he began placing calls. Taking this time to retreat into her room, Sienna opted for a shower to calm her frayed nerves. She found that just being near Matthias brought shivers to her body. Hearing a knock at her door, she left the balcony to answer it.

"Yes?" she asked him, when she opened the door.

"I was wondering if it would be ok if my investigator could come for these documents tonight?" Matthias lifted the files he held in his hand.

"Of course. Anything you need," she told him.

"Thanks. I know it's been a long day, so I will say good night now," he told her. He was about to say more but thought better of it.

"Good night," she repeated, before closing her door.

Sienna pressed herself against the closed door; her heart pounding wildly in her chest. He had showered and changed into a pair of low-riding, gray sweatpants and nothing more. Her eyes had traveled over his bare chest, touching everywhere at once. She had to forcibly resist falling into his arms just to feel his body against hers.

Breathing raggedly, Sienna pushed away from the door. After removing her robe, she climbed into bed, although she knew there wouldn't be much sleeping tonight.

#

Matthias had to forcibly shut his mouth to keep from saying what nearly slipped from it. When Sienna suggested he could have anything he needed, he wanted to tell her he wanted her—in his bed. He knew he didn't have to ask permission for Kobe to come to the suite, but he wanted to see her before he bedded down for the night. Although he had tried to push her from his mind while he got some work done, his mind wouldn't allow it.

He drew his hand down his face, wondering what had come over him. She was his client and he never, ever mixed business with pleasure. He should never have kissed her that first time. Even despite the fact he claimed it was for practical purposes, he knew it wasn't entirely true. He was attracted to her more than he should be. Hearing a slight knock at the door, Matthias pulled his mind back to the business at hand—helping Sienna gain control of her corporation.

Chapter 6

After spending a second tumultuous night, with Matt under her roof, Sienna opted for a day at the spa. This left him and his investigator to dig deeper into her company's holdings. They had opted for breakfast in their suite, instead of in one of the resort's restaurants. At dinner last night, with Matt caressing her cheek and thigh at their table, neither was in the mood to pretend for Romaro Grey's sake. Sienna felt if they had continued their heavy petting this morning, after the night she had dreaming of Matt, she would've asked him to take her right then and there.

They had spent the previous morning at the beach, snorkeling and parasailing. After lunch, they had taken a boat tour along the island, soaking up the sun and the sights. She had a great time with Matt; such a great time that when they sat down for dinner that evening, she had wished their relationship wasn't a charade. She wished they were indeed a couple on a tropical getaway.

Matthias was no better. All night long he lay awake wondering how it would feel to be inside of Sienna. The more he tried to push her from his mind, the more his body demanded her. After fighting his need for her most of the night, he had risen to take a cold shower and dig back into his work. He planted himself up to his neck in paperwork. This is how Sienna found him when she announced she was heading to the spa after breakfast.

#

"Do you think it was wise for you to move in here?" Kobe West asked his boss. He noticed the moment Matthias answered the door that he was wound up tight, and he knew the reason why. Kobe had been employed with Matthias for years and knew his boss well. Not only was he Matthias' employee but also a friend.

"What do you mean?" he asked causally. Matthias didn't look up. He was focused on a document from the files Kobe had brought him. They had decided to have all paperwork from his law office back home faxed to his old suite, which Kobe now occupied.

"I mean, you're here with a beautiful woman who you're obviously attracted to. And from the looks of you this morning, I can see you've been wrestling with living here, physically as well as mentally." Kobe noticed the dark circles that had appeared around his eyes, as well as his bunched shoulders.

"Man Matthias, maybe you should have joined her at the spa for a massage of your own," Kobe suggested with a shake of his head.

Matthias lowered the document and sighed. He had been questioning his plan of moving in with her all night. At the time it seemed harmless enough, but that was before he realized just how near she was to him despite his self-appointed hands-off policy. That same policy that was now mocking him.

"It's not a problem. I'll get through it," Matthias said without looking at Kobe because he didn't know how he was going to get through it without coaxing Sienna into his bed, which he knew was out of the question.

Glancing at his boss once more, Kobe shifted back to work. "It seems that our Mr. Romaro Grey is like a little king amongst the resorts. The staff at all of the locations, either fear him or loath him. There are very few people who fall in between," he told Matthias.

"How so?" Matthias asked. He ignored his stack of spreadsheets to focus on Kobe's evaluation of Grey.

"Well, you would think he owns the corporation the way he strolls around this island. It appears that he gathers information on the staff, information that he uses to control them. While their generous salaries were managed by Pilar Mendez personally, this scum finds other ways to threaten their livelihood if they don't do his bidding. From those who would talk to me, I've gathered that the man may be into other things besides just skimming from the books. Although I haven't seen any real evidence of it yet, there are plenty of rumors suggesting otherwise."

"So the files we received from the accountants, definitely prove he's been skimming from the books?" Matthias asked him.

"Well, it's been proven that somebody has been taking money, but to put Grey's actual hands on it is another story. Because the resorts use an onsite accounting firm, it would stand to reason that someone from that pool would be the guilty party. But as I stated before, Grey is a tyrant here, which could easily mean he's paid someone or is blackmailing someone in accounting to do his dirty work for him." Kobe watched as Matthias thought this over. He knew he was trying to devise a plan to smoke out the corruption.

#

Sienna lay on her stomach, while the massage therapist kneaded her knotted muscles. She relaxed as the anxiety and stress melted away. She never knew that just being near a man could cause so much tension. Matt's presence was wreaking havoc on all of her senses. No man had ever grabbed her attention the way he had.

She didn't know how long she could hold back on her true attraction to him. Whenever they closed the door to their suite, she would retreat to her room as soon as humanly possible without being rude. Rarely did they linger to participate in any casual conversation.

Sighing, she wondered about Matt. Even with the charade, the man appeared to be able to turn his emotions on and off at will, but not her. If he wasn't on the phone, he was meeting with Kobe. Often, whenever Kobe would join them, Sienna would stick around to chat with him. She liked Kobe, especially since his presence eased the sexual tension in the room.

After the spa treatment, Sienna decided to have lunch before her next appointment to have her hair and nails done. She and Matthias had plans to go into the city for dinner and come back later to take in one of the many shows that were available that night.

"Ms. Mendez," Romaro greeted her after she placed her lunch order. The man seemed to have materialized out of thin air.

Was Matt right? Was he following her? "Yes, Mr. Grey? What can I do for you?" Sienna asked, trying not to appear repulsed. She wished Matt was with her. She didn't like to be in this man's presence alone and that dislike was beyond their initial introduction.

"Ah, it's not what you can do for me, but what I can do for you. I was wondering, will you be making any changes in staff after you accept ownership?"

Sienna noticed that his mouth may have been smiling, but his eyes were not. She knew she would have to proceed with caution where this man was concerned. She had already informed Matt that she wanted Romaro Grey to be the first to be let go after the transition. The man gave her the creeps.

"Mr. Grey, I haven't made up my mind one way or another about the staff. If there aren't any major problems, I don't foresee any major changes. But that will all be determined once my attorney finishes his assessment of the resorts and then and only then will I make my final decisions.

Romaro lifted a brow at this, wondering how the man could make any assessment without being present. Without showing it, he was very pleased with the attorney's absence. It was of no consequence to him. The less Stone knew the better it was for him and his lucrative side hustles.

"Well, I'm sure Mr. Stone will find everything satisfactory. I am proud to say I have done my very best at managing the properties. Your mother had the utmost confidence in me and trusted my judgment enough to oversee not only *Sienna's Secret* but the other resorts as well. And I can assure you that I will continue to do the same for you."

Sienna nodded and smiled a smile she wasn't feeling; anything to get the creepy little man to move along. Grateful that he was about to leave, she let out a slow and steady sigh.

"Oh, and Ms. Mendez," he stopped and turned before walking away. "Will Mr. Stone be joining you during your stay?" he added hopefully. It didn't hurt to ensure the man wouldn't be visiting later.

Genuinely smiling this time, Sienna, answered, "No, Mr. Grey, Anderson doesn't need to join me on this trip. I'm certain everything will be fine in his absence," she assured him.

Romaro Grey nodded and left the restaurant with a smug and confident grin. He believed, since Anderson Stone wasn't on the island that everything he had done to cover his tracks was working. Romaro assumed Sienna had faxed the attorney the files she had collected. He felt if Anderson had found the slightest impropriety, he would have flown there in a shot. Romaro was pleased that his inside man had taken his threats to heart. He made it very clear if there were any issues with the books, the man would pay dearly.

Chapter 7

Matthias had chosen Marguerites by the Sea for dinner. This eloquent restaurant boasted a chef's table menu, with their meal prepared table-side. Matthias chose a main course Treasure Coast Grilled Grouper, prepared with risotto, beurre blanc, crab top, and Caribbean salsa. Sienna's dish of choice was Treasure Cay Seafood, a pasta dish consisting of Caribbean seafood, and coconut lime cream. They enjoyed a bottle of chef-suggested house wine and for dessert, gourmet cheesecake served in a pepper sauce. Sienna was in food heaven.

"From the smile on your face, I see that you thoroughly enjoyed the meal," Matthias teased. He had noticed her expression of pure satisfaction as she savored every bite.

"Mmm. I must say that was one of the best meals I have ever eaten," she told him with a well-pleased smile.

"Sienna, have you visited Jamaica before?" Matthias asked, before sipping from his wine glass. Since spending time with her, he noticed she seemed in awe of everything that surrounded them. Although he had been to the island several times before, he still found beauty and mystery in the place.

Sienna shook her head. "No, this is my first time. I've always wanted to visit but didn't see the point if I had to do it alone. This place is truly for couples, for lovers." She was also thinking of the hotel's amenities and how everything catered to lovers.

Too bad I can't take advantage of that part of the package, she thought, as she gazed at Matthias.

"So there is no one back home waiting for you?" he asked. Even though they were pretending to be lovers, he didn't think she would have been quick to agree to the sham had she had a man waiting for her. He was sure that any man involved with Sienna would not have been pleased with the recent turn of events, even if they weren't true. He knew he wouldn't have been.

She shook her head again. "No, no one. With my career, there just isn't much time for a relationship. I've dated a few times over the years, but I haven't come across the man that clicked with me." Until now, she wanted to add but didn't. Sienna felt if there was a man perfect enough for her it would be Matt Bennett. But that was a moot point since she was his client and they were there on business.

"What about you? I can only assume that you aren't married or otherwise Mrs. Bennett would be here ringing my neck, with all the affectionate displays we've been presenting," Sienna chuckled.

Matthias laughed along. "No, there isn't a Mrs. Bennett. Like you, with my career and the traveling that I do…" He shrugged. He had met many women along the way and had tried to make a couple of those relationships work, but like Sienna, no one clicked. One day he would like to settle down and have a family. Each time that he visited his sister with her family or his brother Evan with his new wife, he longed for the joy he witnessed in their lives. Letting his glance linger on Sienna, he vowed someday.

#

Not wanting to call it a night, they opted for a speakeasy-themed party in Margaritaville, instead of catching a show back at the resort. Sienna sighed with relief at Matthias' suggestion; feeling that any time they were anywhere near their suite would be too much temptation to stop pretending. Although both felt the sexual tug, neither was willing to address it; each having their reasons not to awaken the sleeping dog.

With Matthias donning a fedora and Sienna a feather boa, they joined the party atmosphere. The couple danced to the modern-day music encased in the 1920s setting. They were having the time of their lives, with Matthias's hands possessively placed on Sienna's narrow waist or generous hips most of the night Neither having a care in the world. They were having such a good time enjoying the party, and each other, that they never saw Romaro Grey observing them. And Romaro never saw Kobe watching him.

#

When Romaro Grey first learned of Pilar's daughter Sienna, he had fantasized about her in his bed, doing the things that only he could do to her. He had hoped she would visit the resort named after her while her mother was alive and unattached. He believed if he had some productive alone time with her, he would be able to seduce her and maybe even encourage her to marry him.

This would have given him all the access he needed to her entire fortune.

But he never got the chance to meet the woman until after Pilar's death when she appeared to claim her inheritance. He still had high hopes after her mother's demise; sensing the perfect opportunity when she checked into the hotel the night she arrived. But not only had he blown it with his over-eager actions, but she had also brought her own toy to play with.

Romaro learned through staff gossip that the man—this Matt person— had arrived the day after Sienna and had only been with her a few months. He knew the type. Pretty boys who charmed and lived off of rich women. Romaro was sure that now Sienna Mendez was a very wealthy woman, the man would want to stay by her side forever; maybe even persuading her to marry *him*. Romaro knew if he were in the man's shoes, it would be his goal.

Gazing at Matthias, Romaro grew agitated. He watched him caress a smiling Sienna as they worked the dance floor. Romaro followed the couple whenever he had the chance, hoping to find a chink in the man's armor, a way to get rid of him. If Matt wasn't in the picture, he felt he may still be able to coax Sienna to look at him the way she looked at her boy toy.

#

Kobe made note of Romaro's agitation where Matthias was concerned. Kobe didn't like the man. Although he suspected him of shady dealings, he felt there was a lot more that Romaro Grey was hiding. Taking a sip from his drink, he placed his empty glass on the bar top.

Kobe West, a private investigator for Bennett and Associates, was ex-military. At six foot four, two hundred and ten pounds of sculptured muscle, he was in perfect health. With the skin color of heated caramel, a shaven head, and a closely shaven face, he often attracted the attention he didn't seek the moment he entered any room, especially from the opposite sex, and tonight was no different. The moment he entered the club, he grabbed the eyes of most of the women in the place. They immediately took note of his chiseled features, along with his other masculine attributes. Kobe ignored them all. He had work to do.

After Matthias had voiced his concerns that Romaro Grey had been following him and Sienna, Kobe had made it a point to tail them whenever they left the resort. And just as Matthias had suspected, Grey was following them.

Romaro Grey had watched them while they dined and then followed them to the club. Kobe didn't like the way the man was eying Sienna and liked even less the look of pure hatred that he had for his boss. Kobe assumed the man had his own designs for Sienna, which meant Matthias was a problem for him. He didn't know if Grey was dangerous or not, but one thing was for certain, he was going to keep a very close eye on him.

Kobe turned when he felt a present at his side. One of the women had gathered the courage to approach him.

"Hi," she said with a wicked smile as she gazed up at him.

Not wanting to draw suspicious attention from Grey, Kobe decided to engage in conversation with the woman. "Hi yourself," he responded with a well-practiced smile. Even though the woman was attractive, she wasn't his cup of tea.

Extending her hand the woman introduced herself. "I'm Rae Ann, but my friends call me Rae," she told him in her southern twang.

Kobe took the hand she offered for a polite shake. Rae was an attractive full-figured woman with a head full of light brown micro braids, which were styled to perfection. Her makeup was expertly applied, complimenting her clear skin and unique features. She was dressed in a pattern-print strapless dress that hugged every curve as if the dress was made a part of her body.

Kobe admired her assets as he returned the greeting. "Kobe," he said, releasing her hand.

"So Kobe, are you here alone?" Rae asked while she gave the room a visual sweep for a companion that might come along and ruin her chance.

"Yes, unfortunately, I am. My wife wasn't feeling well and insisted that I leave our hotel room to give her some space," he told Rae. Kobe, although not married, had donned a wedding band the moment the plane touched down at the airport. Something he did frequently in his line of work. He didn't want to have to fight off any unnecessary attention while he was working. However, he did find at times that even the ring wasn't enough to deter some women.

Rae pouted. She thought for sure she would have a little fun while she was there on vacation. "Wow, it seems all the good ones are already taken," she told him, once he drew her attention to the wedding band.

Not wanting to appear put off or rude, Kobe chatted with Rae, all the while discreetly keeping an eye on Romaro. He learned that she was from southern Texas and was there on a little bit of business but mostly vacation. He only caught bits and pieces of the woman's conversation, all the while keeping an eye on his surroundings. Kobe laughed and smiled when it was appropriate while appearing to be into Rae as he watched Romaro.

After a while, sensing that Kobe's interest wasn't entirely with her, Rae excused herself and rejoined her friends, just as Romaro headed for the club's exit with Kobe on his heels.

Chapter 8

Romaro Grey watched the couple as they boarded the tour bus for their trip to Ocho Rios. After ensuring the bus was well on its way, he picked up the house phone and rang housekeeping. He had waited long enough to continue his lucrative ventures. He had left the day-to-day handling of his projects in someone else's hands, which was always dangerous, especially with Sienna on site.

Romaro had been unable to personally manage his side business for keeping an eye on Ms. Mendez, while she sifted through the resorts' files. Although he had fully expected the corporation's attorney, Anderson Stone, to accompany her, he was almost giddy to learn that the trusted attorney was not needed on this trip.

Now that the couple had decided to finally spend some time as tourists he could continue to grow his offshore bank account. He knew Sienna and her toy Matt would be gone until late evening, giving him plenty of time to accommodate as many guests as possible.

"I have clients for you to service," he informed the person after the call connected. He rattled off room numbers and times. After giving precise instructions he disconnected the call, smiling. By the end of the evening, he will have cleared close to ninety thousand dollars, after providing the workers their cut.

Romaro had been running a lucrative prostitution ring from the moment Pilar promoted him to Director. It had started by accident after a male guest asked if he could supply girls for a weekend bachelor party. After making a few calls, he connected with an acquaintance he knew back in the States, who made the necessary arrangements. Because of the weekend's success, he had more business than he could have dreamed of and that should have been enough for him. Despite the profits, he decided to add an even more unsavory layer to his new business —blackmail.

Romaro had made arrangements for the exploits of some of his select customers by having them recorded during their time with his special maid service. Not only was he making a bundle with the girls, but he was pulling in double by extorting wealthy men who rather not have those recordings shared with their wives or the media.

Romaro glanced up just as two of the "maids" from housekeeping entered one of the elevators to visit one of the hotel's guests. They both carried small tote bags containing the items that the gentleman had requested. He nodded at them just before the doors closed. Quickly peering around the lobby, Romaro grinned as he mentally counted his money.

#

Kobe waited in his suite for his "guests" to arrive. He couldn't believe Matthias had talked him into this. He was all for catching that scumbag Romaro with his hands in illegal activities, but he wasn't certain that his participation in said activities was a good idea. While he had a way out, he was still nervous as hell about the whole situation.

Kobe had stumbled upon Grey's prostitution racket by accident. He had been probing around at the *Daybreak Beach Resort* when he overheard one of the male guests asking the concierge if there was any female action to be had for the night. From the looks of him, the older man was rearing to go too. Kobe shook his head at the thought of the old guy trying to keep up with a much younger woman. But then again, there were those little blue pills.

He mentioned what he had discovered to
Matthias, who promptly came up with this plan. A plan
he was now about to execute.

Kobe chuckled at the sham Matthias himself was
involved in. His boss was about to climb the walls from
his pretense with Ms. Mendez. Each time he met with
Matthias, he noticed the darkening circles around his eyes
from lack of sleep. It would've been great had it been
from bed play. But Matthias's problem stemmed from not
revealing his attraction to Sienna and letting the chips fall
where they may. He shook his head again. He warned
Matthias that he was playing with fire and now he was
paying the price.

Kobe's grin turned into an instant frown at the
knock on his door. Drawing a deep breath, it was show
time.

#

Bria Talbert sat in the stairwell of the hotel, while
she waited for Kobe's signal. He was to send her a text
when it was time for her to play her part of the angry
wife. She thought Kobe was joking when he asked her to
fly down and join him with this sting. They both had

worked for Matthias for the past five years but had never worked together on any of the same cases. So when he suggested she come to Jamaica to assist him, she was thrilled—until he gave her the details of the job.

Bria has had a crush on Kobe from the moment she met him. She was glad that it was only a crush or she may not have been able to work this job with him. She hid her attraction well because she knew, as a woman, Kobe didn't know she was alive. Although there were times when she caught him staring at her, he never showed any emotion, so she just accepted his view of her as just another colleague, nothing more.

Feeling her phone vibrate, she looked at the screen; it was show time.

#

After waiting until the agreed-upon time frame, Bria quietly let herself into the suite. Making her way to the bedroom, she readied herself for the performance of a lifetime. Counting to three, she stomped into the room and let loose an ear-piercing scream.

"OH MY GOD! What the fuck is going on in here?!" she screeched. "Is this why you were in such a hurry for me to go shopping, so you could get your rocks off with these hood rats?!" Bria loudly hurled accusations at Kobe while the startled women froze in place, unsure of what to do next.

There they all were, with Kobe in boxer briefs and the two half-dressed women perched on either side of him. The sight of the trio was so comical, that it took everything within Bria not to burst into laughter before she could complete her dramatic performance.

Shoving the humor to the side, she ramped up her performance by removing her earrings and kicking out of her red-bottomed Christian Louboutin pumps to fight the stunned women. "Which one of you bitches wants her ass beat first, huh?" Bria growled as she lunged at them.

The two women finally snapped to their senses and scrambled from the bed to grab their clothes, while trying to avoid Bria's swinging fists. Amid the chaos, Kobe had gathered the totes the women had brought with them. They were so anxious to leave that they didn't dare take time to grab them. After pulling on enough clothing to leave the suite without questioning stares from any guests who might be in the corridor, the two women ran for their lives.

Bria, after making sure the two sex workers had left, double-locked the door, just in case they realized they had left their bags and wanted to return. She smirked at the thought. She doubted the two would come within a thousand feet of the room after her performance.

"What took you so long?" Kobe asked her when she returned to the bedroom. He was zipping up his jeans.

Bria rolled her eyes. "It only took me a couple of minutes, Kobe. It wasn't like you were naked when I arrived, geesh."

"Well a few more seconds and that grabby blonde would have had me out of my boxers," he countered, irritated.

"Yeah, yeah, yeah…did we get anything good?" she asked when he tossed her the two totes.

"I believe so. After the fake blonde helped me out of my shirt and pants, the other girl pretended to reach for condoms, but I saw her cell phone instead. I'm sure she took photos." He started to put his shirt back on but changed his mind, and tossed it on a chair instead.

Rummaging through the bags, Bria found the phone. Scrolling through the photos, she found three of Kobe and the crew, along with photos and videos of other unfortunate victims. Tossing the phone to Kobe for his examination, Bria plopped down on the foot of the bed.

Blowing out a sigh, she looked around her at the disheveled bed and Kobe's scowl, after he viewed himself on the woman's phone. She grinned when she recalled the look of terror on the women's faces when she rolled up ready to issue them a beat-down. Bria started to chuckle at first. But the more she thought about the chaotic scene the more she laughed. Soon she was laughing so hard, that she fell back onto the bed holding her midsection.

While she was lying there entertaining herself with laughter, Kobe took note of Bria's attire. Aside from the breast-hugging blouse she was wearing, Bria wore the shortest skirt that he had ever seen her in. The more she rolled around on the bed, the further it crawled up her thighs.

Bria was twenty-seven years old and sexy as hell. Kobe had noticed her immediately after she joined Matthias' team of investigators. She was petite but shapely. Her hair was a silky, shiny sandy brown, which she always wore long and straight. He often fantasized about entangling his fingers in her hair. She always dressed nice and wore impossibly high heels which he believed compensated for her barely five-foot stature. Today was no exception; except for the shorter than short mini skirt.

Tossing the phone in the chair with his shirt, Kobe joined her on the bed. She was laughing so hard, that she hadn't noticed he was lying beside her until she felt his warm palm on her upper thigh. Reigning in her amusement, Bria turned her head just in time to see Kobe's lips coming for hers.

Instead of questioning the moment, Bria moaned and went with the flow. She ran her hands over his bare back, as his hand traveled further up her thigh, removing her panties and then her skirt.

Leaving her lips to stare into her eyes, Kobe waited for any signs of resistance before removing her blouse and bra, freeing her full breasts. Bria's eyes were hooded with desire as she gazed back at him with only acceptance.

Receiving his answer, Kobe lowered his mouth to kiss and suckle each breast, as he entered her with fingers that caressed and branded her as his own. Listening to her shallow panting, he continued his sensual assault on her body, until he rose from the bed, only long enough to remove his pants and underwear and retrieve the box of condoms from one of the workers' bags. Kobe donned the protection before returning to a fully aroused Bria.

"I've wanted to do this for so long," he breathed into her ear, just before he entered her with one smooth stroke.

Bria heard his declaration, but she would have to rejoice later. For now, she would let him love her into oblivion.

#

Why didn't you let me know you were attracted to me?" Bria asked Kobe. They had spent the better part of the afternoon attending to each other's desires.

Kobe kissed her before he answered. "I didn't think it was appropriate, because we worked together," he told her as he held her closer. Kobe was more than attracted to her. He had fallen for her years ago.

He had wanted to take her out on dates and do all the normal things that most men did when they were interested in a woman. But he wasn't most men. His job often took him away from home for days, sometimes weeks at a time. Every time he got up the nerve to let her know how he felt, a new case came along either for him or her. So when the opportunity came for them on this trip, he didn't hesitate to invite her.

"I hate to point this out, but we're working together now…on the same case, I might add. So what changed? Here we are in a hotel room, where we all but tore the place apart." Bria was overjoyed that he was attracted to her, but she wanted details.

"It's because we are in a hotel room, on this beautiful island. Ever since I got here, all I could think about was you; that you should be here with me in this paradise. So when this opportunity came up…" Kobe shrugged. He hoped his answer would satisfy her. He wasn't ready to reveal his true feelings just yet. Kissing her again, but more passionately this time, he reached for the last condom.

#

After copying everything that they needed from the phone, Bria continued her role as the irate wife. She stormed down to the lobby, loudly asking for a manager. What she got was Romaro Grey.

"Yes, Miss? Can I help you?" He asked her.

"It's Mrs., and yes you can help me by keeping those skanks away from my husband." She threw the totes at him and rolled her eyes, before sashaying for the elevators.

Romaro waited until he entered his office and closed the door, before dumping the contents of the totes onto his desk. Searching through the items, he found what he was looking for. He closed his eyes and breathed a sigh of relief.

When the girls had come rushing back down frightened and without their belongings, he nearly panicked. He hurried them into his office where he discovered the client's wife had returned to the suite early. He was angry that they left without getting the phone. He was worried that it would fall into the wrong hands. Not knowing what to do, he knew he couldn't very well march up to their room asking for the bags. He would have to wait to see what transpired next.

After scrolling through the photos, Romaro was grateful that the woman was too caught up in her husband's deception to be concerned about the contents of the bags. Finally relaxing, he tossed the phone into a drawer, locking it. He was relieved that he was back in control.

Chapter 9

Matthias held onto Sienna's hand as they climbed up Dunn's River Falls. They were having a great time on the tour. He thought they should indulge in some fun, while his staff back home was poring over the books among other things. He knew Kobe had things under control back at the resort, so he felt they were overdue for some relaxation. Besides, he felt as if he would lose his mind if he hadn't gotten away from any place that had a bed. The pretense that he and Sienna were perpetrating was getting to him. The more time he spent with her in their shared suite the more he wanted her. So when the concierge suggested the tour, he jumped at it.

"This is more fun than I could have imagined," Sienna told him when they stopped to pose for photos along the climb. Some of the guides took photos of the climbers at various points along the falls for later purchase.

"I must say I agree. As many times that I have visited the island, this is my first time at the Falls. It's breathtaking."

Finally making it to the top, they headed back towards their tour bus. The Falls were their last stop on the day-long tour. They had enjoyed horseback riding along the beach, visited the Nine Mile village, the birthplace of Bob Marley, and taken a history tour of the island and its people.

When they reached the tour bus, they were met by their driver. "I am very sorry folks, but we are having some mechanical problems and won't be able to return to Montego Bay tonight." There was grumbling from the crowd. "But the tour company will put you up in one of the local hotels here in town. So if you will follow me, I will take you to the hotel shuttle."

#

Sienna and Matthias exchanged glances after they entered their small cramped hotel room. They both immediately noticed there was only one king-sized bed. Because of their appearance of being a couple, they had no choice but to accept the room that was assigned to them. The only other furniture the room held was a table and two chairs for dining. Matthias felt the Fates were mocking him with this new arrangement.

"You take the bed and I will make do with the chairs," Matthias told Sienna.

"Nonsense. The bed is big enough for the both of us, we're adults, we can sleep in the same bed for heaven's sake." Sienna's voice boasted more confidence than she was actually feeling. How was she going to sleep with Matthias in the same room with her, let alone the same bed?

Resigned to his fate Matthias nodded. "There are some shops still open, why don't we go get some things that we'll need for the night and grab some dinner," he suggested. Turning on her heels, Sienna followed him from the room.

While Sienna shopped for toiletries and other items for their overnight stay, Matthias checked in with Kobe.

"How did things go today?" he asked his number two man.

"We were right. There is a prostitution ring, along with some blackmail in play here, but it's going to take a bit more work to find out who's all involved. When I made arrangements for the girls, I spoke with a female, so

Grey has others doing the front work. I just need to connect the woman to him."

"Do you have any idea who the woman is?" Matthias asked.

"I have some idea, but I will have to do some more digging to make sure. The biggest question is, how are you going to survive an entire night in one room with Ms. Mendez?"

Matthias closed his eyes and swiped his hand down his face while he thought over Kobe's question. How was he going to survive it? The woman wanted them to sleep in the same bed for Christ's sake. How was he going to manage that without touching her?

"I don't know man, I don't know." Matthias thought about hiring a car to take them back to the resort but changed his mind. If they wanted to catch Romaro Grey with his hands dirty, they would have to give him enough time to slip up. With him and Sienna away, the man would relax and maybe show his hand.

#

"Are you comfortable?" Sienna asked Matthias once he climbed onto the other side of the bed.

After shopping for their overnight needs, they decided to order some food to take back to their room. They had engaged in small talk while they ate. After dinner, Matthias left to give Sienna some privacy while she prepared for bed. When he returned, he found her already in bed, with the only light in the room glowing from the television. Ducking into the bathroom, he opted for a cold shower to fend off any present and future arousals he may have during the night. It didn't work.

"Yes." Sighing, Matthias turned onto his side with his back to her. They each had claimed the edge on their side of the bed, for fear of accidentally touching.

"If the television is bothering you, you can turn it off," Sienna informed him. She didn't know what else to say or do. She had never been put in a situation like this before.

"No, it's fine." Matthias was gritting his teeth. Whatever fragrance she was wearing was driving him crazy.

"Well, good night."

"Good night," Matthias returned.

\#

"Good afternoon, I hope you had a pleasant trip despite the tour bus breakdown." Romaro Grey greeted them when they entered the lobby.

"Good afternoon," Matthias greeted the man with a face-splitting grin. Sienna smiled and nodded. Matthias had her hand firmly clasped in his as they headed for the elevator.

Matthias couldn't recall a worse night than lying next to Sienna, unable to touch her, since their meeting. Most of the night had been spent fighting a constant threat of an erection that prevented him from getting much sleep. He didn't know when he dozed off, but when he awoke the next morning, he found himself pinned under a tangle of Sienna's arms and legs, which were casually thrown over him as if it were the most natural thing in the world.

After boarding the elevator, Sienna leaned against Matthias and rested her head on his shoulder. Although they were to assume they were under constant surveillance by Romaro, she was just exhausted and saw no reason not to lean against him. Once they entered their suite, Sienna headed for her room and a nap, while Matthias checked in with Kobe.

Closing her door, she released a breath she hadn't realized she was holding. It had been pure torture to sleep in the same bed with Matt and not have him make love to her. When they had awakened, she found herself nearly on top of the man. Horrified she scrambled from the bed apologizing profusely. She had retreated into the bathroom where she had showered and dressed. Too embarrassed to leave the bathroom, she was relieved to find, once she had emerged, that he had left the room to find their tour guide. She couldn't look at him for the rest of the morning until he told her some corny joke to break the new level of tension that had formed between them.

Sienna dropped onto the bed exhausted. She only meant to close her eyes for a second but fell fast asleep. The previous night's ordeal had been too much.

Chapter 10

After dinner, Matthias found himself pacing the length of his room. He had retreated to his bedroom the moment they cleared the door to their suite. He didn't know how much longer he could pretend to be doing Sienna when all he wanted to do was plunge himself deep inside of her.

He thought he could handle the kisses and making out that they had engaged in, for the sole purpose of continuing their subterfuge. But it was becoming more difficult to keep the charade going without the constant cold showers afterward. Their little display in the elevator a moment ago had nearly sent him over the edge. He knew if he didn't get away from her immediately, he would have taken her right there in the doorway. And he wouldn't even allow himself to think about the night before in Ocho Rios when they shared a bed.

Matthias blew out a long sigh in frustration. Not knowing what else to do, he stripped off his clothing, opting for another cold shower before he found himself storming Sienna's bedroom to tear off her clothes.

#

Sienna had come into the common room to grab some fruit. She had just changed into her nightgown for the night and assumed that Matthias was in his room. After they returned from dinner, he told her he had a few calls to make and had retreated into his room, closing the door firmly behind him. She was a little disappointed but understood.

In the elevator ride up, they had made out like a couple of teenagers, after bumping into Romaro in the lobby. He had been eying the guest activity inside the elevators from the monitors at the front desk. Although he was cordial enough as they strolled through, Matthias knew the hateful man still watched them.

Once on the private elevator which led directly to the floor of their penthouse suite, Matthias had backed Sienna into a corner, kissing and caressing her wildly. Giving whoever was watching every indication of what they should be doing, once they reached their suite. Sienna could feel his erection protruding into the apex of her thighs, signaling that indeed he wanted her as much as she wanted him. But to Sienna's disappointment, the moment the door closed behind them, Matthias instantly retreated to his room. It was just as well she thought. After all, once the properties were transferred, they would part ways. She wasn't sure she wanted just a casual fling.

When Sienna rounded the corner, she collided with Matthias. "Oh, I'm sorry Matt, I thought you were in your room," she told him. Had she known she would run into him, she would have dressed more appropriately or at least donned a robe. She was wearing a sheer, short scrap of a nightgown that barely hid her body from his gaze.

Matthias had reached out to steady her but released her once she took a step back. "I just finished my shower and came out for a bottle of water," he explained. The shower hadn't helped, so he thought maybe some ice-cold water would do the trick.

"Well, I'll let you get to it." Sienna gave him a weak smile, before turning to leave.

Matthias reached for her then; preventing her from retreating into her room. He'd had enough of the cat-and-mouse game they had been playing with each other. Sure they had pretended to be lovers for the sake of his investigation, but he wanted to make it true. Every time he kissed her or caressed her, he wanted to take her back to his room and undress her. He needed to feel her bare skin brush against him as he moved inside of her.

Pulling her to him, Matthias lowered his mouth to hers. Sienna closed her eyes as she anticipated his lips meeting hers. She knew this kiss would be different. They were not out in public putting on a show for Romaro Grey. They were in the privacy of their suite where there would be no barriers to stop them from completing the act they both had been pretending wouldn't happen.

Matthias's tongue parted Sienna's lips as his mouth gently pressed against hers. He pulled her more firmly into his arms as he molded her body into his. He assaulted her senses; exploring her mouth with his tongue. Sienna moaned her answer to the question that his mouth had asked—did she want him? Matthias took this as permission to press his erection into the V of her thighs, letting her feel without a doubt that he intended to grant her request.

Lifting her into his arms, Matthias headed for his bedroom. He gazed at her through passion-filled eyes, as he hurried them to his bed. Placing her there, he watched while she slowly pulled the skimpy night dress she was wearing over her head, tossing it to the floor. He swallowed, while he gazed at the breasts he had admired the first time he saw her. From there he let his gaze travel to her narrow waist and then to her rounded hips that cradled what waited for him.

Matthias quickly removed his clothing before joining her on the bed. Before covering her with his body, he opened the bedside table's solitary drawer, to retrieve a condom from the box he had purchased the day before; anticipating this very moment. He knew after spending the night in the same bed in Ocho Rios, it was inevitable that he would love her before leaving the island.

Applying the protection over his generous erection, he covered her body with his. He tasted her mouth, and her breasts; barely able to control himself as Sienna moaned and thrashed under him. Finally obeying his body's command to join them, Matthias lifted her legs and pulled her bottom against the front of his thighs. He attempted to enter her, only to be met by an unexpected barrier. His eyes widened at the realization of what was happening. Sienna did have a secret—she was a virgin. Not knowing how to respond to this turn of events, Matthias attempted to pull away.

"No! Don't!" Sienna stopped him by encircling him with her legs; trapping him in place. "Don't stop," she commanded in a passion-filled voice.

"Sienna, maybe we should discuss—" Matthias began, only to be cut off by Sienna's mouth devouring his.

With her legs and arms wrapped firmly around him and her tongue deep inside his mouth, he felt he had no choice. Again he entered her, but this time with gentle thrusts, to not harm her tender flesh.

Easing in, all the way through the barrier, Matthias rested his forehead on her shoulder; waiting while her body adjusted to him. Sienna had tensed only for a moment, absorbing the shock of her body being entered for the very first time. Feeling body her relax, Matthias began to move inside of her; slowly at first; still not sure if he was doing the right thing. He never expected her to be a virgin. But after his body demanded he get on with it, he picked up the tempo, thrusting faster and deeper, swerving his hips as he cried out at her body's tight fit around him.

Each thrust brought them both unimaginable sensations that threatened to incinerate them. Matthias lifted her hips, driving deeper inside her. He couldn't believe how good she felt. Sienna moved with him, chanting his name repeatedly with each thrust. Not able to hold on any longer, her walls gripped him tighter as he drove her over the edge. They both cried out at the force of the shared orgasm. Breathing rapidly, Matthias rolled off her, bringing her with him to lie on his chest.

"Why didn't you tell me?" he asked, after a long moment of silence. After their joining, his mind had been racing as to how to handle the aftermath of the situation.

Sienna lifted her head to look at him. "I didn't think it was important. I wanted you, you wanted me," she told him a matter-of-factly. That wasn't true; she knew if he discovered she was a virgin, he wouldn't take her. They had been touching each other too much for that not to happen.

Sitting up, Matthias turned to look at her. "Sienna, that was important—your first time…" He didn't know what else to say.

"What would you have done differently?" She asked him. "Would you not have made love to me?"

Matthias thought about this. He didn't know how to answer her questions. What would he have done differently? Lying back down, he pulled her back into his arms. He would have to think about that one.

But before he could form any answers, Sienna leaned up and parted his lips with her tongue. Abandoning his search for those answers, Matthias rolled over to enter her again.

#

Opening his eyes to glance at the bedside clock, Matthias could see that it was still early. He turned to look at a sleeping Sienna. He smiled at the thought of all the things they had done during the night. Although she had been a virgin when he first took her, Sienna was a fast study and had caught on quickly. If he hadn't known for sure that she was new to making love, he wouldn't have believed it. She was uninhibited, willing to try anything he suggested. Just thinking about all the positions and motions that they had indulged in, gave him an erection of steel. He would let her sleep. He knew her

body was sore and needed a break. Pulling her closer to
him, he drifted back to sleep.

Chapter 11

Needing to gather the final documents for the upcoming meeting, Matthias left *Sienna's Secret* after lunch to drive to his make-shift office in his old suite at *Pilar's Playground*. Before leaving, he kissed Sienna, promising to meet her later for dinner in one of the hotel's finer restaurants. The audit had come to its conclusion and it was time to celebrate. While looking forward to the end of his investigation, he wasn't looking forward to them parting ways. He had grown very fond of Sienna and wanted to continue to spend time with her once they left the island.

The only problem with them keeping in touch was the inconvenience of not living in the same state. Matthias had shrugged and promised himself that the minor issue would not become problematic. He would find a way to make it work because he had no intention of allowing Sienna to walk out of his life. Before they were married, his brother Evan had successfully worked out his long-distance relationship with his wife Jean, so the solution shouldn't be difficult to achieve.

After spending their first night together as actual lovers, Matthias and Sienna spent every moment alone in bed. He worked by day and they enjoyed each other by night. They saw no reason to venture out every evening anymore, trying to avoid the inevitable and the need to put on a public display for Romaro Grey's sake. The conclusion of their audit and investigation had freed them all from secrecy.

Matthias's team was certain they had gathered all the evidence needed against staff who participated in the uncovered financial theft and the illicit sex-for-hire operation. Now that the investigation was complete, it was time to formalize the transfer of power and cleanse Sienna's corporation of its corruption.

With Matthias's assistance, Sienna arranged a meeting with her company's local managerial staff, including resort concierges, accountants, and managers for the following morning. The summoned teams from all five resorts were to meet in a designated conference room at the flagship resort, along with island police. Matthias would then unveil his true identity and announce all changes and arrests. He, along with his US team, had quietly hired trusted replacements for each removed staff member. Those new hires would instantaneously step into their roles once the meeting was called into order.

Arriving at his destination, Matthias brought the Jeep to a stop. Smiling, he vowed to make the errand quick so he could return to Sienna.

Chapter 12

Romaro Grey paced the dusty floor trying to come to grips with his predicament. He hadn't intended to grab Sienna, but she had angered him by laughing at his advances. That was the last time that she would rebuff him, he thought. The last time.

At a rare moment, he had caught her without her constant companion, Matt. He was taking a shortcut back to his office, through one of the private gardens, when he came upon her taking in some sun and admiring the ocean view. Viewing this as his opportunity to make his intentions known, he approached her.

Since the night Sienna arrived, Romaro had watched her. Following her and her guest just to capture a glimpse of her. Sienna was a beautiful woman, and with her wealth and power, she could open doors for him. Doors that were always locked to people like him. He had plans for the resorts, that included expanding the themed hotels to other islands—along with his other ventures, of course. But he needed control of her company to fulfill his dreams.

Romaro Grey was born and raised on the island of Jamaica near Port Antonio. He had grown up in poverty and watched visitors from other countries live a life of luxury and ease—a lifestyle he longed for. Even the poorest of the Americans who visited his homeland appeared to possess the sort of life that he was lacking, as well as so many others who inhabited the island. Once he became old enough to work at the resorts, he vowed he would succeed and become one of the elite whom he served. He would not let poverty become an obstacle that would keep him from possessing and enjoying the life he so desperately wanted and believed he deserved.

After graduating at the top of his high school class, earning him a free ride to a prestigious university in the US, Romaro worked and studied hard to obtain his Master's degrees in both business and finance. He understood that acquiring the money and power he desired would take a great deal of skill and knowledge. He believed it would be enough, but soon learned that it was not. There was an abundance of ambitious people on the fast track to succeed as he was. The growing competition made it difficult for him to find a position that would catapult him to the status he longed for—that was until he discovered the ideal position offered by The Mendez Corporation.

Romaro submitted his résumé and credentials and waited with not much hope that he would be accepted. He fully expected to be rejected as with all the other positions to which he had applied. But to his surprise, he was contacted for an interview and thereafter granted the position. Although it was located back on his island home, he eagerly accepted his new appointment as senior manager for the corporation's flagship resort *Sienna's Secret*. Effectively applying his knowledge and skill, he advanced quickly, capturing the attention of the corporation's head and owner Pilar Mendez. With Pilar's respect and admiration, he was soon placed as director over the entire group of resorts.

Romaro smiled at this memory. He had worked his ass off to ensure the coveted position was his and he had made it happen. Pilar Mendez was pleased with his work and trusted him completely. With the new lucrative position, he had made more money than he dared dreamed, but still, it hadn't been enough.

"If I had just been content with that honor," he whispered to himself, while he continued to pace the length of the dilapidated floor.

He glanced back across the room at a still unconscious Sienna. He swept his hand over his head, returning his thoughts to the impossible situation he had landed himself. He hadn't meant to hurt her. He just wanted her to see how good they could be together. But when he suggested they meet for dinner and discuss future plans for her company, she had laughed at him.

It wasn't her laughter alone that angered him, but the pure unadulterated disgust that had appeared on her lovely face. How dare she think she was too good for him when she was sleeping with that worthless piece of trash? A man who slept with wealthy women for a living. At least he had a respected livelihood, unlike her boy toy Matt.

With Sienna's blatant rejection, Romaro angrily lashed out by punching her in the face, rendering her unconscious. He quickly glanced around to see if they had been observed. Not seeing any witnesses to his callous behavior, he hurriedly carried her through the private garden through one of the hotel's service entrances, where he quickly hid her in a large laundry cart. Not knowing what else to do, he brought his car around and placed her inside the trunk; driving her to a small abandoned shack; a shack where he and his family once lived.

After Romaro was established as head director, he had moved his parents from the dreaded dwelling into a modest but comfortable home on the other side of the island, far from the memories of hardship that had plagued them there. Although no one lived there anymore, he couldn't bring himself to have it destroyed. He needed it as a reminder of where he came from and where and how he would never return to live again.

Deep in thought, of the past and the present, Romaro's head whipped around when he heard a moan come from the makeshift bed. Sienna was coming around. She had remained unconscious even after he lifted her from the trunk of his car and brought her into the shack. After placing her on the bed, he tied her hands to a post near her.

He had to think. What was he going to do with her? If she only would see him as a worthy mate, someone who could grow the corporation with her by his side. Drawing a deep and ragged breath, he moved to Sienna's side as she opened her eyes.

Awake, Sienna tried to lift her hands from their awkward position only to find them bound above her head. Quickly looking around the room she spotted Romaro stalking towards her. Instantly panicking at what she remembered, she screamed.

"Scream all you want, no one can hear you here," he told her in his thick native accent.

He sat beside her on the bed, with Sienna scooting away from him as best she could. Romaro caressed her cheek with the back of his hand. "I could make you happy if you would only allow me," he told her, as his hand moved from her cheek to her neck. Horrified, Sienna drew away from his touch. Angry, Romaro stood from the bed to look down on her.

"Why won't you try? What's wrong with me that you won't even consider a life with me? Do you prefer that trash that you roll around in bed with over me? The man isn't anything more than a common whore, moving from woman to woman for his bread and butter. I have a life, and prestige at the resorts—on this island! People here look up to me," he sneered, pointing at himself. "With my knowledge and your power, together we could take the corporation to any level we choose!" Romaro was drunk with rage and the unrealistic power he craved.

"What are you going to do with me?" Sienna asked. She swallowed as she waited for his answer. She had no intentions of feeding into this madman's unrealistic fantasies.

Sienna's thoughts focused on Matthias. What must he be thinking after returning to the hotel and not finding her there? Would Romaro be his focus once he discovered that she had been taken? And if so, how would he know where to look for her? She didn't even know where she was. Since Matthias had everything under control, she saw no need to accompany him and had stayed behind to wait for his return. She now wished that she had joined him.

Once everything had been resolved, Sienna was more than ready to celebrate. They had planned a nice dinner and afterward, they would dance the night away. The thought of being able to breathe easier knowing by the end of their meeting, Romaro Grey would be behind bars. She had been more than ready to witness the hateful little man's arrest. But the moment that would bring her the most enjoyment would be Romaro Grey's bewilderment once he learned of Matthias's true identity. But now, she didn't know if she would survive to see any of it to fruition.

Anticipating what was to transpire at the meeting the following morning Sienna had gotten restless and decided it was time to visit her mother's suite. She had put it off long enough. Taking the keycard, she walked the short distance down the corridor to Pilar's domain. Sienna drew in a calming breath before she slid the card into the lock, disengaging it.

Stepping inside, she closed the door and forced herself further into the room. The suite was similar to hers, but she recognized her mother's touches all over the place. She noticed that just as her home had been decorated and furnished with expensive taste, so had Pilar's home away from home.

Sienna walked around the room touching everything, as she imagined Pilar doing so. She wanted to feel a connection to her. Making her way into the master bedroom Sienna stopped short at the photos she saw of her with her mother and of Pilar alone. These images brought tears to her eyes. Picking up one of the framed photos from the dresser, she stared at a laughing Pilar before hugging it to her chest and collapsing to the floor into deep sobs. She hadn't allowed herself to grieve until that moment. She missed her mother so much.

After her emotional release in her mother's suite, Sienna had ventured outside into one of the private gardens. She had only been there for a short time when she encountered Romaro Grey. The man had startled her, but she deemed him harmless just the same. She felt confident knowing that he would soon be arrested and put away. That was her mistake. She had been so confident that she had laughed at him when he suggested they get together for dinner. That was all that she remembered. With her jaw painfully throbbing, she now found herself in her current predicament; tied to a bed with this lunatic looming over her.

Leaning over her, Romaro touched the swollen side of her face only to have her jerk away from him again. "If I was the low-life that you think me to be, I would strip you bare and prove what a man like me could offer you. I am a better man than that Sienna."

Romaro shook his head in disgust and walked over to a dirty window. "I could never take a woman against her will. That is not who I am." He used a corner of his shirt to clean a spot on the upper pane of the window. Focusing on the surrounding brush, he listened to the nearby surf crashing against the rocky shore.

Sienna quietly released a slow ragged sigh of relief. She was sure he would try to force himself on her. While his back was turned, she took the time to inspect the room. The walls were nothing more than worn boards nailed together to form the dingy space. There was a doorway to her left that she assumed led to another room. The room they were in held the bed and a chair nothing more. She looked up at the ceiling which was also just boards nailed together, coated with what appeared to be tin. She wondered what was this place.

Turning, Romaro noticed Sienna taking in her surroundings. "This is my childhood home," he told her. "There are exactly three rooms. This room is where I and my brothers slept. My parents had the other room and there," he pointed beyond the doorway," is where my mother prepared our meager meals."

Spotting something, Romaro frowned. Without warning, stalked over to the doorway to snatch down some cobwebs that had gathered there. More agitated than ever he turned and glanced once more at Sienna, before leaving and locking the door behind him.

Sienna, feeling this was her only chance to escape, twisted and turned trying to free herself from the bondages, but to no avail. She would just have to wait and hope that Matt would find her.

Chapter 13

Anderson Stone's eyes narrowed as he listened to the grim news coming from the other end of the phone. Even though it had appeared that Pilar Mendez had died of an apparent heart attack, it was routine for the coroner to run various tests just to be thorough. It had never entered his mind that her death could be anything more than natural causes. But here was a detective telling him otherwise.

Anderson drew his hand down his face while he listened to the details of Pilar's death. She had been poisoned. A deadly compound was used to trigger the heart attack. After thanking the man for the unexpected information, Anderson disconnected the call. Overwhelmed, he thought of the implications and the complications that this could pose for Sienna, not to mention Matthias.

Matthias thought his greatest problem would be catching someone looting the coffers, not murder. Because he was no longer involved with the case, Anderson had been kept out of the loop in most of Matthias' findings. He wondered if the same person who was skimming money was also responsible for Pilar's death or the very least somehow linked to her company. From his perspective, Pilar's death had to be due to some business disagreement, because she was as gentle as they came without an enemy in the world.

Picking up the phone again, he knew he had to warn Matthias. Sienna could very well be in danger. If the killer took out her mother because of the company, he or she wouldn't think twice about targeting Sienna. He dialed Matthias' number only to reach his voicemail. Anderson left an urgent message requesting a return call. Placing the phone back on its cradle, all he could do now was wait. But if Matthias didn't call him back immediately he would continue calling until he reached him. This was life or death.

#

"Have you seen Sienna?" Matthias questioned Kobe after he finally answered his pounding on the door.

When Matthias arrived back at their suite, he expected to find her there waiting for him. At first, he wasn't concerned. He just assumed she had gone down to the lobby or maybe to one of the boutiques. But once he emerged from his shower and had dressed and she still hadn't appeared, he became worried. He had called the front desk to see if the staff knew of her whereabouts, but no one had seen her.

"No, what's the matter?" Kobe asked as Matthias pushed past him. He begrudgingly closed the door after Matthias stepped further into the room.

"What's going—" Bria started, wandering from the bedroom while tying her robe. "Oh, hi Matthias," she said with a blush at having been caught nearly naked in Kobe's suite.

After taking in Bria's attire, Matthias finally noticed that Kobe was standing there in his boxers. Kobe and Bria had been indulging in a little celebration of their own.

"Oh, look you guys I'm sorry," he apologized; running his hand over his hair. "Sienna is missing. We were supposed to go to dinner when I got back from *Pilar's Playground,* I've looked everywhere but she's nowhere to be found. All of her things are still as she left them…her purse, phone…only her keycard is missing." Matthias was upset.

"Why don't you head downstairs, we'll be right down," Kobe suggested. "Matthias, we will find her."

Heading for the door, Matthias nodded in agreement. They had to find her.

#

"Did you ask the staff if they had seen her?" Kobe asked when he and Bria reached Matthias at the front desk.

"No one has seen her all day," he told them.

"Ok think. What did she say just before you left…anything specific?" Bria asked, hoping that he may have forgotten an errand or trip that she may have taken.

"No, nothing."

"Ok, let's split up and comb the grounds and the other four resorts," Kobe told them. They made arrangements to check in if they found her or not every hour.

#

While Matthias was upstairs with Kobe and Bria, Romaro had slipped back into his office unseen. He sat at his desk, contemplating what to do with Sienna. He couldn't keep her there forever. He was sure her lover had missed her by now.

Romaro wasn't really worried about Matthias and since Sienna's only immediate family was deceased, he could get her to sign everything over to him then she could have an unfortunate accident. He displayed a small smile at this thought. The smile was quickly replaced by a frown when his door swung open bringing an anxious Matt inside.

"Grey, have you seen Sienna today?" Matthias asked the frowning man.

Romaro was beyond angry that Matthias had rushed into his office without knocking, but managed to conceal his rage to listen to Matthias's rantings. "Why no, what's the problem?" he asked as if he didn't already know.

Matthias ran his hand over his close-cropped hair, as he explained not being able to find her. Romaro assured him that she had to be on the grounds somewhere and had offered to help look for her, but Matthias rejected his offer, to his disdain. Before Matthias left, he asked him to keep his eyes open and let him know if he saw her. Romaro had nodded, anxious to get rid of the man.

Even though he hadn't voiced it, Romaro knew Matthias believed he had something to do with Sienna's disappearance. He even had the nerve to ask where was he the first time he had come to inquire about Sienna's whereabouts. Romaro told him that he had been out tending to some tasks out on the grounds. Although Matthias seemed to be appeased for the moment, Romaro knew he would be back when he wasn't able to locate her.

He smiled again. If his luck held, the hateful man would never see Sienna again.

Chapter 14

Romaro's eyes widened as he listened to Sienna's disclosure. He began to shake with fear that was coupled with rage.

After he informed Matthias that he knew nothing of Sienna's disappearance, Romaro had planted himself at the front desk, curious as to what the man would do next. He wanted to gauge the concern of her lover now that he had discovered her missing. Matthias's discomfort had brought Romaro great satisfaction watching him on the verge of panic because he couldn't find his beloved Sienna.

While he watched Matt pace the lobby, his curiosity was piqued further after the irate wife who returned the sex worker's belongings emerged from one of the elevators. With her was a man who he assumed was her husband. The two joined Matt as if they knew him. He couldn't hear what they were saying but he knew the conversation had to be about Sienna's disappearance. They conversed for a few minutes more before the trio left the hotel, undoubtedly in search of Sienna.

Romaro didn't know what to make of the three. He had never seen them together before. Were they working together to scam the young heiress out of her money? Or was there something deeper going on? He had to know. After the group left, he carefully made his way back to the shack; making sure that he hadn't been followed. Once he was inside, he questioned Sienna immediately.

Now learning that her so-called boy toy was actually Matthias Bennett, her estate attorney and the two people with him were private investigators, he was beyond stunned. He was so convinced that he had nothing to worry about when Anderson hadn't appeared to attend to her estate that he missed what was right in front of his face. It never occurred to him that there could be another attorney involved. He just assumed Stone was lazy and incompetent.

Romaro paced the floor wildly as he tried to think of the implications of what could happen. Did they already know about his ventures with the prostitutes and the blackmail? He didn't know but he bet Sienna did.

"How much do they know?" he asked when he finally stopped pacing to consult her. He had untied

Sienna from the bed but kept her hands bound as a precaution. She sat on the cot eating the food he had brought her.

Romaro returned with food and water along with several battery-powered lanterns, which hung from nails protruding from the walls. The sun was beginning to set.

Sienna stopped chewing her jerk chicken long enough to answer him. "They know everything; the prostitution, the blackmail, who your accomplices are," she told him defiantly. She was glad to see him rattled for once. If he was shaken enough, he would make mistakes, mistakes that could free her from this madman.

Placing the bowl to the side, she stopped eating to watch Romaro. For the first time since meeting the man, fear had taken over him, fear that had left her unsettled. At least now she knew Matt was out looking for her, that much gave her some hope. Hope was all that she had with the uncertainty of her future in this unhinged man's hands. And with that hope, she prayed Matthias would find her in time.

Romaro continued to pace, placing both hands on top of his head. He was screwed. He couldn't go back to his home, the hotel. He was sure by now they had the authorities watching the airport. There was no way for him to escape. He felt like a trapped animal.

Stopping suddenly, he sat down on the only chair the room held and leaned forward, pulling a rather large metal box toward him. It was another one of the items he had brought with him on his return to the shack. He opened the box and pulled out a semi-automatic rifle along with a handgun.

With the introduction of the weapons, Sienna's eyes widen. She understood that she was in more danger than ever.

#

Kobe and Bria watched with concern as all of the color drained from Matthias's face as he listened to the caller on his mobile phone. Neither liked the expression that had settled there—it was fear. Fear was something that neither of them had ever witnessed from Matthias since they started working for him. This was bad.

They each had combed the resorts and grounds, talking to staff members, trying to find Sienna. After checking in several times, they decided to meet back at

Sienna's Secret. Just after they each had given their report, Matthias' phone rang. Kobe and Bria stood and watched as their boss's eyes widened with whatever was being relayed to him over the phone. After Matthias had listened for a while, he told the caller that Sienna was missing. Matthias agreed with something, nodding his head in unison with his spoken agreement then he disconnected the call.

Placing a hand on the back of his neck, Matthias lowered his head and squeezed to try to relieve some of the tension that had settled there. He swallowed before lifting his head to meet his employees' gaze.

"That was Anderson. It seems that Sienna's mother, Pilar, had not died of a simple heart attack. She was poisoned. She was murdered."

Kobe and Bria exchanged glances but did not interrupt him.

"Anderson believes Sienna is in great danger. He's flying down tonight to help with the search." After Anderson learned Sienna was missing, he informed Matthias that he would be catching the next plane out.

Matthias was worried more than after learning of Pilar's murder.

"It's time to get the local authorities involved, we need help," Kobe gently suggested. Matthias nodded. Kobe clasped his shoulder before stepping away to place the call from one of the hotel's phones.

"We will find her Matthias," Bria reassured him.

He could only nod.

Chapter 15

Anderson breathed a sigh of relief once he approached his destination. As soon as he clicked off with Matthias, he dialed another number. He had to get to Jamaica as soon as he could, and the only way he could accomplish that was to call in a favor from one of his clients. The man owed him big time for saving his butt in a multi-million dollar deal that would have gone horribly wrong had Anderson not stepped in. The client had been so grateful for the rescue that his gratitude included a favor needed at any time; all Anderson had to do was call. So Anderson was calling. He needed the man's private jet.

#

Anderson Stone stared out into the night, as the hired car made its way to *Sienna's Secret*. After gaining clearance, for the use of Kincaid's corporate jet from Rowan Kincaid, he had driven to the airport in record time. He needed to be in Jamaica to help locate Sienna. He somehow believed the entire situation was his fault.

He had convinced himself he should have suspected foul play in Pilar Mendez's death. Particularly since they spoke the day before she died. Pilar had mentioned she needed advice concerning some issues with the company. Agreeing, he made arrangements for her to come to his office the next morning to discuss her concerns. Pilar never made it. She died that night of what he and everyone else had believed was a heart attack. Anderson shook his head. It would be all his fault if something happened to Sienna because he felt he should have known better.

As soon as the car came to a halt, Anderson climbed out and rushed toward the entrance of the resort. Matthias met him as he made his way to the front desk.

"Anything?" Anderson asked Matthias.

He shook his head. "No, nothing. We've called the local authorities in. They are looking in places we wouldn't think or know to look," Matthias informed him, clearly worried.

"What about Grey? I know you expressed some concerns about him," Anderson asked.

"That's just the thing. He was here earlier and I questioned him about Sienna, but now he is nowhere to be found. The police have tried him at his home, his folks, even at the other resorts, but he seems to have vanished."

Anderson's stomach began to tighten into knots. He didn't have a good feeling about the man. After learning of Pilar's murder, he was beginning to wonder if Grey was involved. So before he left Metro City, he asked his friend and investigator, Tor Hudson, to check on some things for him. Remembering Tor, he needed to check in to see if he had found anything.

"Excuse me," Anderson told Mathias, as he pulled out his phone to call Tor.

Matthias nodded as Anderson stepped away to make his call. From the moment that Sienna disappeared, he had an uneasy feeling that Romaro Grey was involved. Even though the man was there when they first started searching for Sienna, he still held him as a suspect now more than ever, since he too had disappeared.

Hearing hurried footsteps coming his way, Matthias turned to see Kobe dragging an angry woman towards him. He wondered what this was all about. From the grim set of Kobe's jaw, Matthias figured he didn't have long to wait to find out.

Propelling the woman forward, Kobe ordered her to speak. "Tell him," he gruffly commanded the woman.

Snatching away from Kobe, she turned to glare at him. "I should have known you were trouble," she spat at him in her deep southern drawl.

Sensing the woman wasn't about to speak, Kobe spoke for her. "Matthias, this is Ms. Rae Ann McEwen. Rae Ann is Grey's partner in crime, namely the prostitution and blackmail business," Kobe informed him. "It appears they know each other from college," he further stated while eying the pissed-off woman.

"You see Rae here runs a supposed maid service back in Texas. Whenever a concierge contacts Romaro with guests' requests, he contacts Rae with specific times and dates. She flies a crop of girls down for pre-orders; have them do their business then leave. She only allows a few to stick around for orders put in for same-day service. Once the orders can be filled, the concierge will then contact the guest with a number to call to make the

financial transaction through a credit card, charged to
Roadhouse Services, Rae Ann's *maid* service." Kobe
glared at the despicable woman.

"I'm betting the only reason she's here taking
orders on the island, instead of her comfy distance in
Texas, is because Grey wanted to distance himself from
the operation while Sienna was here, leaving all of the
dirty work in her hands," he concluded with barely
contained contempt.

He and Bria had tracked Rae Ann down and
dragged her kicking and swearing to *Sienna's Secret*. She
had made such a commotion that Bria was standing
outside trying to cool down before she punched the
woman.

"It's lucky for us that she decided to come to
Jamaica on 'vacation', he emphasized, "or we may have
never found her."

"I met her the night you and Sienna were partying
in Margaritaville. At the time, I didn't pay too much
attention to her. But when I called the number given to
me by the hotel concierge to pay for the hookers, guess
whose country ass voice was on the other end taking the

order." He looked at Rae with disgust. "There was no way to mistake your Texas accent," he told the fuming woman, mocking her in a southern drawl of his own. She only rolled her eyes.

Without warning, Matthias grabbed the woman by the upper arm, squeezing tightly. "Where is he? Where is Grey?" He asked her in a low lethal voice with a menacing glare to match.

"Ow, you're hurting me," the woman howled. This only made him squeeze harder, bringing more protests from Rae Ann. Kobe feigned interest in a nearby potted plant, while his boss conducted his business with the irate woman.

"Lady, and I use that term loosely, I'm going to show you what real pain is if you don't tell me what I need to know," he growled at her."

While staring into the woman's eyes to make sure she understood how serious he was, he was unaware that Anderson had finished his call and had joined them. Grabbing Anderson's arm, Kobe stopped him from intervening on the woman's behalf.

After what seemed like an eternity, Rae Ann finally told him what he wanted to know. The group learned that Romaro Grey had a small shack near the other end of the island that he liked to go to from time to time to be alone.

From Anderson, they also learned he had been in the States recently, more specifically at Pilar's home the night she died. Tor had tracked him from the airport through a taxi service he had taken to and from Pilar's home. They were more than certain that Romaro Grey murdered Sienna's mother.

With the additional information Rae had given them about the operation, Kobe placed a phone call to have all the others involved rounded up before they got wind of what was going down. He didn't want any of them disappearing as Romaro Grey had. Kobe had just about enough of this crew and their schemes.

After Bria joined them, and the police had Rae Ann in custody, the group, along with the local authorities, set out for Romaro Grey's shack. They just hoped that it wasn't too late.

Chapter 16

Romaro Grey closed his burner phone with a snap. The call should have worried him but it didn't. He was already trapped.

"I killed your mother you know," he idly informed Sienna without preamble. He didn't see why he shouldn't tell her. He didn't see how he was going to escape the justice that was coming for him. Everything he had constructed was unraveling.

Romaro shook his head at his colossal mistake. Even though he questioned Anderson Stone's absence in settling Pilar's affairs, he should have realized that rich people never did anything half-assed when it came to their money. Of course, she would have an attorney present and he now knew that attorney was Sienna's assumed lover. Romaro almost laughed at the fact that they had gotten one over on him. And to think, he only saw the man as a leech.

"What?" Breaking into his thoughts, Sienna asked him in stunned disbelief. He had to be lying. Her mother died of a heart attack, the coroner said so.

"I killed your mother," he repeated. He sighed and stood up from the chair he was sitting on and moved to the window. It would be daylight soon. And soon they would be coming for him.

"She found out what I was doing and wanted me to resign, but I had other ideas. I figured if I could get rid of her..." he trailed off with a shrug. He turned to look at a horrified Sienna. He gave her a half sneer before telling her why and how he did it.

#

Romaro had been enraged when Pilar happened upon his enterprising side business which he ran out of *Sienna's Secret*. Although he had clientele at the other hotels, *Sienna's Secret* was his headquarters. He had just returned from dealing with a difficult customer at one of the other resorts when he spotted Pilar marching his way. She had arrived the previous day unexpectedly, affirming that she needed some relaxation. It never occurred to him that she was following up on a complaint issued directly to her, by one of the men he was blackmailing.

The man had visited the resort along with some others for a convention. He had heard of Romaro's services and asked for the deluxe package, which included several of his girls for an all-nighter for him and one of his colleagues. After doing some research, Romaro discovered that the gentleman had obtained his wealth and status through his wealthy wife. He saw a perfect opportunity to gain more money from him through blackmail. So while the man was out attending one of the day's many meetings, he had hidden cameras strategically placed in his suite.

Unbeknownst to Romaro, the guest was a close friend of Pilar's. So after he approached the man with his proposition to exchange money for the recorded video, the man immediately contacted Pilar.

Before confronting him, Pilar had smiled sweetly until they reached his office. After the door closed, she tore into him, threatening to expose him and his operation if he didn't turn over the man's blackmail material and resign immediately. Pilar would have gone to the authorities that night if he hadn't given her the man's video and persuaded her to let him dismantle everything before leaving quietly. She had given him one week to accomplish the task or she would turn him in to the police. Pilar had boarded a plane that very night, and returned home, confident that the matter was resolved.

Romaro had much to lose. He paced his office that night, sorting through his options. Sure he could hand over everything and disappear quietly, but his greed had gotten the better of him. And Pilar hadn't known about his skimming of the books, for which she would surely have gone straight to the authorities once this was discovered. Forming a plan, Romaro called Pilar and agreed to bring everything to her by the end of the week.

He had gone to Pilar's home as planned, but instead of handing over the agreed-upon material, he had spiked her drink when she stepped away to answer a call. Although he had given her the supposed files she asked for, they contained nothing more than regular operation reports for the resorts. Romaro was not worried when he left, because he knew she would be dead within the hour and no one would be the wiser.

Looking back into the past, Romaro was trying to discover where he had gone wrong. He had resisted using locals for just this reason; to prevent the opportunity to be caught. All of his girls were high-dollar professionals from the States. They understood discretion and made a decent living off of it. Once their job was done for that trip they would fly home and send a fresh wave of girls, rarely staying more than a few days. He found if they hung around too long, especially at the other resorts, the staff would start asking questions. The girls were known as his special maids. They took care of the things the regular hotel staff couldn't handle. Although most of the staff at *Sienna's Secret* suspected what was going on, they never talked for fear of losing their jobs or worse.

Romaro's eyes narrowed when he thought of the one staff member who had threatened him if he didn't cut him in on the action. A couple of days later, the man had an "accident", by taking a curve too fast, plunging to his death over a cliffside road. He had smiled when he returned to work the next day and saw fear in the eyes of his employees. They had known without a doubt that the man's death was no accident.

Now to learn from an acquaintance in the States that Pilar's death had now been ruled a homicide, Romaro and grown numb. He never expected this. If he had, he would have covered his tracks better. He shook his head.

After all the plotting and planning, in the end, he was the one who messed up.

He glanced over his shoulder at Sienna and casually observed her sobbing over her mother's untimely demise. He rolled his eyes and sighed; turning back to peer out towards the unkempt trees and brush. The sun had risen and as usual, it was a beautiful day. He was about to leave the window when he caught movement in the corner of his eye. He saw several men moving towards the shack. Quickly grabbing the rifle he had propped against the wall, he waited until they came within range and without warning, he started firing.

Frightened, Sienna quickly rolled off the bed onto the floor. She covered her head as best she could as the bullets started flying.

Chapter 17

After the gunfire ceased, Matthias ran to Sienna, pulling her into his arms. He had been so frightened for her. With Romaro shooting like a crazed lunatic and the police returning fire, he wondered if she had been hit.

As soon as Romaro fell to the ground after being struck by several bullets, Sienna waited only seconds after the crack of gunfire ceased, before she bolted from the shack, right into Matthias' open arms. They were about to kiss when a wail that was so deep and so tortured broke the silence, that it immediately grabbed everyone's attention. The dreadful cry made the hairs on the back of their necks stand out.

Mathias, not knowing what caused the awful noise, pushed Sienna behind him to protect her. They both looked in the direction of the sound to discover its heart-wrenching source. Kobe was kneeling on the ground clutching a motionless Bria in his arms, with his tortured soul crying out in agony. She was gone.

\#

When the group arrived at the shack, Romaro had fired shots at them without notice. They all took cover as they tried to get a fix on his position. Kobe and Bria fled in opposite directions of the shack with him crouching behind some boulders and her behind a stand of trees. Each, along with the local authorities fired back at Romaro, praying not to hit Sienna, if she was still alive. The gunfight only lasted a few short minutes before Romaro was struck down.

While everyone else rushed the shack, Kobe tore off in search of Bria, after she failed to emerge from the trees. He didn't have to go far before he found her lying on her back barely breathing. Her chest had been torn open by several bullets. He ran to her immediately, lifting her into his arms. She stared at him in wonder and with love, trying to tell him how much she loved him. But all she was able to churn out were clumps of blood flowing from her mouth and tears from her eyes, catapulting Kobe into action. He ran.

He had only covered a few feet with her cradled in his arms when she drew in her last breath and closed her eyes. Kobe fell to his knees moaning a sound so deep and sorrowful, that it brought instant hurt to those who witnessed it. He knelt there for what seemed an eternity, rocking back and forth, holding onto Bria, sobbing deeply.

Sienna turned to Matthias, buried her face in his chest, and cried.

Epilogue

Seven Months later

"I'm surprised he came." This was Matthias. He was discussing Kobe's presence at the wedding reception with his new wife.

After Bria was killed, Kobe retreated within himself. He had stopped receiving assignments and wouldn't receive or return anyone's phone calls or visits. He was hurting and everyone understood, but they still worried about him. When Sienna sent the invitation, she never really expected him to show. But he had.

"Hi," Kobe greeted when he reached the couple. "Congratulations you two," he continued with a kiss on Sienna's cheek and a shake of Matthias's outstretched hand.

"We're so glad you could make it," Sienna told him. She beamed with joy at seeing him. While he looked a little gaunt with the loss of some weight, he looked better to her than he had the last time she saw him— cradling Bria's body. Hugging him, she excused herself to mingle and to give the two men time to talk.

"Matthias, I want to apologize for skipping out on you like that. I know you needed me, but I just wasn't any good to you in the shape I was in."

"Don't apologize. You know I understand. How are you, really?" Matthias asked his friend.

"I'm…making it. Really, I'm better. I just miss her so much, you know?" Kobe sighed. It had taken him seven months to bring himself to join his friends. It was the first step; the first of many he hoped.

"I would like to come back to work. I've been out of commission long enough. I think it's time."

Matthias nodded. "After the honeymoon my man; after the honeymoon." They both laughed.